NO DOGS ALLOWED!

To my cousin Eddie "Gua Gua" Rivera,
who shared many of these trips with me.
—S. M.

For Adelaine, who loves dogs of all sorts.
(I'd also like to thank my unruly angels, Niko and
Bonnie, for their help.)
—J. M.

E
318-6122

Atheneum Books for Young Readers
An imprint of Simon & Schuster Children's Publishing Division
1230 Avenue of the Americas
New York, New York 10020

Text copyright © 2004 by Sonia Manzano
Illustrations copyright © 2004 by Jon J Muth
All rights reserved, including the right of reproduction in whole or in part in any form.
Book design by Abelardo Martínez
The text of this book is set in Cantoria.
The illustrations are rendered in watercolor.

Manufactured in China
First Edition

10 9 8 7 6 5 4 3 2 1

Library of Congress Cataloging-in-Publication Data
Manzano, Sonia.
No dogs allowed! / written by Sonia Manzano ; illustrated by Jon J Muth.—1st ed.
p.   cm.
Summary: When Iris, her family, and the neighbors take a trip to Enchanted Lake,
everyone brings what they think is needed, but the family dog turns out to present a problem.
ISBN 0-689-83088-2
[1. Automobile travel—Fiction. 2. Puerto Ricans—Fiction. 3. Dogs—Fiction.]
I. Muth, Jon J, ill. II. Title.
PZ7.M3213 Tr 2002
[E]—dc21   00-042022

story by
SONIA MANZANO

NO DOGS, ALLOWED!

illustrated by JON J MUTH

Atheneum Books for Young Readers • New York London Toronto Sydney Singapore

Hi.
My name
is
Iris.
I'm seven.

And once, a long while ago, when I was six, I lived in a place called the Bronx, in the Kingdom of Third Avenue, in the Land of New York City, with . . .

. . . a big sister named Shorty the Fortune-teller, who could tell the future by rolling her eyes;

. . . a mother named Mami the Busy, because she was always busy doing something;

. . . a father named Papi the Clever, who, with the touch of a hand—and about five or six hours—could fix anything;

. . . and a dog named El Exigente, because he didn't do a thing.

One day we decided to go to the lake in the Enchanted State Park.
We woke up very early (that's how you beat the traffic and get a good
picnic table). It was so early it was still dark outside.

It was so early I had extra trouble waking
El Exigente because he's very good at sleeping.

My Mami the Busy and my Papi the Clever got everything ready. Mami made a little lunch and a little after-lunch snack. Then she made a little dinner and a little after-dinner snack. *Then* she made dessert and a little something for the road, in case we got hungry.

My papi packed, saying, "Only take what you know you'll really need to go on a picnic."

My big sister Shorty
the Fortune-teller packed
a few essentials.

DOG
FOOD 50 lb.

And I was packing for El Exigente when my sister yelled,
rolling her eyes, "MOMMMMM! Iris can't bring that dog, can she?
There'll be nothing but trouble if he comes!"

"There'll be nothing but trouble if he stays," said my mami.

We lugged our things to the sidewalk and met . . .
. . . my cousin Carmen the Beautiful. She brought her
    traveling beauty parlor;
. . . my other cousin, Marta the Smart. She brought a few books;

. . . my Aunt Tuta the Happily Married and her Brand-new Husband,
    Juan. They were so in love they could only bring each other;

. . . Don Joe the Grocer, who brought his deli counter;

. . . the Wise Old People, who wisely brought a table, chairs, and
a box of dominoes so they could finish a game they started one
hundred years ago when they were young in Puerto Rico;

. . . and a few neighbors from the tri-state area. They brought things too.

We loaded our trucks and cars and trailers, and off we went. We never took the highway. Papi said old roads were better to break down on.

Which we did.

"I knew we were going to break down," said my big sister Shorty the Fortune-teller, rolling her eyes.

"That's okay," said my mami. "We can have a snack, and it gives me a chance to crochet a nice cloth for the picnic table."

"And it gives me a chance to rotate the tires after I fix the car," said Papi cleverly.

"And I can fix my hair a bit," said Carmen the Beautiful.

"And I'll have time to finish reading this Grimm fairy tale," said Marta the Smart. "I was just getting to the good part."

"And I'll be able to make some sandwiches to have before, during, and after we get to the lake," said Don Joe the Grocer.

My Aunt Tuta the Happily Married and her Brand-new
Husband, Juan, gazed into each other's eyes and said, "Oh boy!
This gives us a chance to spend some time together before we get
to the lake to spend even MORE time together."

The Wise Old People didn't say anything, but looked around wisely, set up
their table and chairs, and broke out the dominoes.

Anybody who wasn't changing a tire, looking for a car jack, or crawling
under their car, got busy preparing a snack for anybody who *was* changing a
tire, looking for a car jack, or crawling under their car.

Anybody left over got a chance to do whatever they wanted to do.

I got a chance to play tug-of-war with El Exigente. He was very good at that.

So I knew exactly where the road map was
when my papi wanted to check it so we wouldn't
get lost once we were on the road again.
   But we got lost, anyway.

"I KNEW we were going to get lost," said my big sister Shorty the Fortune-teller, rolling her eyes.

"Think of it as an adventure," said my mami. "Besides, it gives us a chance to visit other neighborhoods and practice our English when we ask for directions."

One day we actually got there. "It's a miracle," said my big sister Shorty the Fortune-teller.

I couldn't wait to do all the
things I'd been thinking of, like
jumping in the Enchanted Lake and
getting some enchanted sun and
eating some enchanted lunch
and taking an enchanted nap and
building some enchanted sand
castles . . .

. . . and that's when my big sister's eyes stopped rolling long enough for her to read the enchanted sign that read: NO DOGS ALLOWED! (enchanted or otherwise).

"I knew it! I knew it! I knew it!" She was hopping mad. "I knew this was going to happen!"

I gulped. My sister was right! El Exigente DID cause trouble! This was terrible! What were we going to do? Go home after breaking down and getting lost because El Exigente was a dog? He couldn't help it. He was born that way. Besides, being a dog was what he did best! Why weren't dogs allowed at the lake, anyway?

I looked at Mami. My mami and papi looked at each other. Everyone started talking at once. In English and in Spanish.

Then Papi said, "Wait a minute, can you all be quiet so we can figure out what to do!?"

"We'll never figure out what to do!" said my sister, rolling her eyes. But everyone was too busy trying to figure out what to do to hear her.

Then my papi yelled, *"CALLENSE!"* at the top of his voice. (This means, in case you didn't guess, "QUIET!" in Spanish.)

And then he thought for the longest minute of my life.

Finally, he said cleverly, "Look, these packages are heavy—we might as well put them on a nice picnic table until we figure out what to do."

And then my mami got busy, saying, "It's hot. I might as well mix some coconut-pineapple punch and set out the blankets in a nice, shady spot until we figure out what to do."

And Carmen the Beautiful said, "I might as well put on my swimsuit in case Prince Charming shows up until we figure out what to do."

And Marta the Smart said, "I might as well go make some fairy tale sand castles until we figure out what to do."

And Don Joe the Grocer said, "We might as well eat those sandwiches I made until we figure out what to do."

My Aunt Tuta the Happily Married and her
Brand-new Husband, Juan, had decided to put their
heads together and take a walk around the lake to
try to figure out what to do.

And the Wise Old People had already wisely
sized up the situation and found the perfect tree to
play dominoes under until somebody else figured out
what to do.

Then Papi the Clever said,
"We should takes turns staying
with El Exigente in the parking
lot until we figure out
what to do."

PARKI

So that day, in the parking lot of the Enchanted State Park, my dog had his fur done by Carmen;

. . . was read to by Marta;

. . . was fed by Don Joe;

. . . was baby-sat by my Aunt Tuta and her husband, Juan;

. . . played dominoes with the Wise Old People;

. . . had his paw read by my sister;

. . . and was hugged and kissed
by me until we could figure out
what to do.

And before we knew it, it was dark. My cousin Marta the Smart couldn't read anymore. Aunt Tuta and her Brand-new Husband, Juan, were anxious to get home to start becoming an old, happily married couple. Carmen the Beautiful had put rollers back in her hair, plus—there was nothing left to eat. It was time to leave.

And as we drove home, El Exigente and I agreed that my sister Shorty the Fortune-teller was right, both times. El Exigente DID cause trouble, and we never DID figure out what to do.

But it didn't matter because we both felt tired and sleepy and happy and sandy, just like you should feel after spending the day at the Enchanted State Park.

THE END